Sandy Claws AND Chris Mouse

written by

Lois and Ray Shope

Illustrated by Michael White

Flutter-by Productions

Written for the child in all of us.
Dedicated to our children and grandchildren; and with gratitude
to the family of Stella and Peter Thomas.

In loving memory of Alice & Lawrence

Flutter-by Productions
1404 Goodlette Road North, Naples, FL 34102
www.flutter-byproductions.com

FIRST EDITION

Shope, Lois.
    Sandy Claws and Chris Mouse / written by Lois & Ray Shope ; illustrated by Michael
White. -- 1st ed.
    p. cm.

    SUMMARY: An orphaned kitten and his mouse friend live in the Nativity stable and
discover a special gift that only they can offer the baby Jesus.
    Audience: Ages 1-6.
    LCCN 2004111403
    ISBN 0-9714734-0-4

    1. Jesus Christ--Nativity--Juvenile fiction. 2. Gifts--Juvenile fiction.
    [1. Jesus Christ--Nativity-- Fiction. 2. Christmas--Fiction. 3. Gifts--Fiction.
    4. Cats--Fiction. 5. Mice--Fiction. 6. Stories in rhyme.]
    I. Shope, Ray. II. White, Michael, 1964- ill. III. Title.

    PZ8.3.S55916San 2005   [E]

              QBI05-600110

The illustrations were created in mixed media. The text type was set in Garamond.

Printed in the United States of America

Book design by Tim Cameresi

On a night long, long ago,
this legend first began.
It's the story of two good friends
and God's great gift to man.

The hero of this fable
defies all natural laws,
for this champion
of little mice
was a cat named
Sandy Claws.
His fur was
sandy colored.
That's where he
got his name.
What he did
for others
was how he
won his fame.

A fluffy little kitten,
without friends or family,
the shelter of a stable
was his only luxury.

Hunting for his food at night,
he learned skills to stay alive.
Sandy lived all by himself
and was able to survive.

He often watched the little mice.
He heard laughter as they played.

But when he tried to join them,
they'd run away afraid.

"What's wrong with me?" he would cry.

"Why do they run away?"

He didn't want to frighten them.

Just longed to join their play.

Then one day, he heard a scream
outside his little stall. He looked and there
was Mrs. Mouse trapped against the wall…

...surrounded by evil rats, there was
no time for pause!
He leapt in front of Mrs. Mouse
and bared his sharpened claws!

Although he was outnumbered,
Sandy showed no fear at all!
He bowed his back! Hissed through his teeth!
Stood there brave and tall!

Confronted by this fearless cat, the rats were terrified!
They scurried out the stable door!
They took off far and wide!

Little mice came running out from every nook and cranny, happy that their Mom was safe and giving thanks to Sandy.

"Thank you, dear!" said Mrs. Mouse. "I really didn't know that a cat could be our friend instead of just a foe."

Mrs. Mouse adopted him.
She raised him
like her own.
The mice became
the family that
he had never known.

That made Chris
his brother.
He was a friendly
little mouse.

He showed Sandy a hiding place in the tree outside their house.

When Chris hid in its big branches, he was impossible to see.

That's why all the animals called it the *Chris Mouse Tree!*

One cold and bitter winter's day,
just as night began to fall,
Sandy Claws and Chris Mouse
were huddled in their stall.

Suddenly, they heard a noise
and the doors blew open wide!

A man came in the stable with a
donkey by his side.
Riding on the donkey and
clinging to its mane
was the man's expectant wife,
a woman in great pain.

He gently helped her
to the hay and then
as he was done…

...the cat and mouse
stared in awe
and watched the
birth of her new son.

At that
very moment,
a bright star
lit up the night...

...shining through
the darkness
to shed a
peaceful light.

The babe was wrapped in linens.
A manger was his bed.
Shepherds came
singing praise.
"Joy to the World!"
was what they said.
The little child
slept on in peace.
He did not even stir
as three kings
honored him
with gold,
frankincense
and myrrh.

"What child is this,"
Sandy thought,
"that kings would seek to find?"
"This is the Son of God,"
they said,
"the hope
of all mankind."

When the kings had gone away,
while Mary and Joseph slept,
Sandy said, "Let's take a peek."
So silently they crept.

As they reached the manger, the baby cooed and smiled.
It was then that they both knew the wonder of this child.

"We have no gifts that we can give,
nor praises we can utter."

Then the wind began to howl.
They saw the baby shudder.

Sandy quickly looked at Chris.

They had a gift to give!

Warm, soft fur could block the cold
and help this child to live.

So they climbed into the manger
and slept there through the night.

When the parents looked at dawn,
they found a precious sight…

Sandy Claws and Chris Mouse
and a warm little baby boy
in the manger, sound asleep.
Their hearts were filled with joy!

Just outside the little stable
was another special sight!
Animals from everywhere
had gathered through the night.

Some had hung red berries
on limbs wrapped in frosted snow.
Little birds flew 'round the tree
tying gold and silver bows.

They had trimmed the
Chris Mouse Tree while singing songs
of cheer. It's a wonderful tradition
that we now repeat each year.

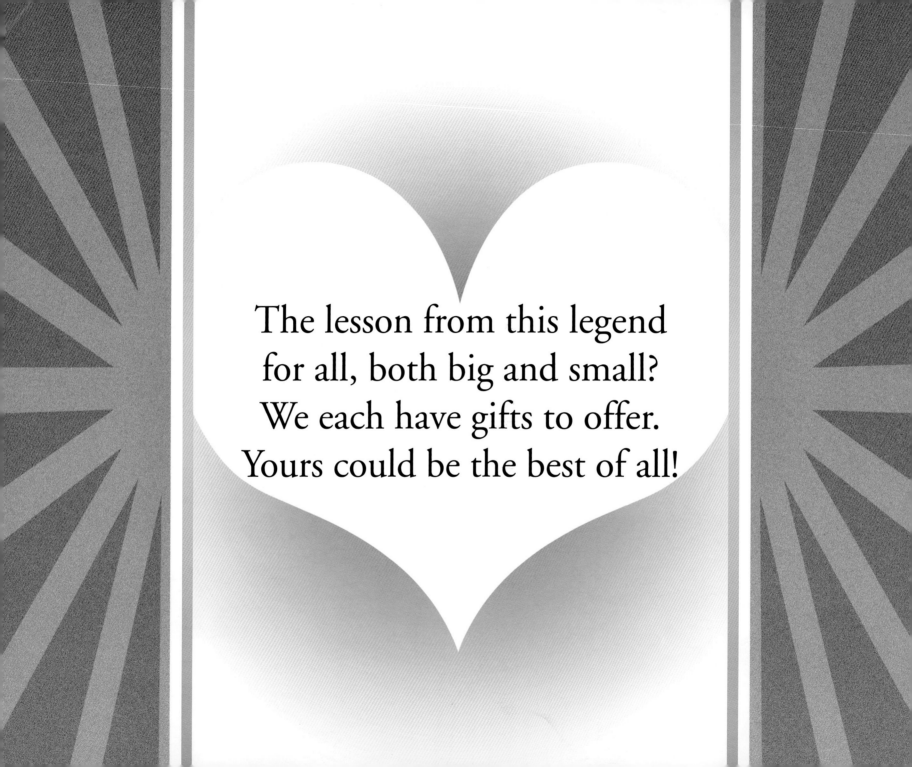

The lesson from this legend
for all, both big and small?
We each have gifts to offer.
Yours could be the best of all!

The Beginning